This edition published by Parragon Books Ltd in 2016

Parragon Books Ltd
Chartist House
15–17 Trim Street
Bath BA1 1HA, UK
www.parragon.com

Adapted from the teleplay by Ursula Ziegler Sullivan
Illustrated by Harry Moore

ISBN 978-1-4748-4295-2

T#488414

Printed in China

The Pups Save Christmas!

Bath · New York · Cologne · Melbourne · Delhi
Hong Kong · Shenzhen · Singapore

It was the day before Christmas. The PAW Patrol pups were decorating the big pine tree outside the Lookout.

"These old tennis balls will make great decorations," Chase said.

He pushed a lever on a small catapult that Rocky had made and launched a green ball up on to a branch.

"I love Christmas," said Zuma. "I can't wait for Santa to get here."

When the pups were finished, the tree looked beautiful, but they all agreed that something was missing.

"A star!" Skye exclaimed. Wings popped out of her Pup Pack as she grabbed a golden star from the box of decorations. Skye zoomed up into the air and placed the star on the top of the tree.

Later that night, Ryder watched his Santa Tracker on the Lookout's viewing screen. It showed a big blizzard on the horizon – and Santa was flying right into it!

"Don't worry," Ryder said. "If anyone can fly through a bad winter storm, it's Santa."

But at that very moment, Santa was having trouble. The storm rocked his sleigh back and forth. Bags of presents fell out, and a big golden star slid off the sleigh. Santa and the reindeer landed hard in the snow.

Back at the Lookout, Ryder received a call on his PupPad. It was Santa!

"My sleigh has crashed, and I've lost a lot of gifts," Santa said. "My reindeer are missing too. Worst of all, my Magic Christmas Star is gone. That's what gives my sleigh and reindeer the power to fly! I need you and the PAW Patrol to help me save Christmas."

Ryder gathered the pups together. "Rubble,
I need you to help dig the sleigh out of the snow."
"Rubble on the double!" Rubble shouted.
Ryder looked at Rocky. "I need some recycled
parts to fix Santa's sleigh."
"Don't lose it – reuse it!" said Rocky.

Ryder continued. "Skye, Zuma and Marshall, I need your helicopter, hovercraft and fire truck to help deliver gifts to Adventure Bay."

"This pup's got to fly!" Skye exclaimed.

"Let's dive in!" Zuma cheered.

"I'm fired up!" Marshall called out.

"And Chase," Ryder said, "I need your megaphone and net to help round up Santa's reindeer."

"Chase is on the case!" Chase shouted.

"All right! PAW Patrol is ready to roll!" Ryder said, and all the pups raced away from the Lookout.

Ryder, Rocky and Rubble found
Santa's sleigh in the snow. Rubble got
to work digging it out with his shovel.

When he was finished, Rocky rolled his truck into position and lifted the sleigh. Ryder saw that one of the sleigh's runners had snapped. "We'll have to replace it," he said. "Rocky, see what you have in your truck."

While the sleigh was being repaired, Skye zoomed through the blustery night, looking for the lost bags of presents. Her searchlight scanned the dark forest below. "I see a bag," she reported to Chase and Marshall. "Can you pups pick it up?"

The bag was stuck in a tree, so Marshall used his truck's ladder to climb to the top. He reached up to grab the bag. Suddenly, he slipped off the ladder, and the bag tumbled down, too.

Chase quickly launched a net to catch the falling bag of gifts. Marshall landed in the soft snow.

"I'm okay!" he said with a smile.

Skye, Chase and Marshall found the
other bags of gifts and met Ryder at
the sleigh. Rocky attached an old ski
to the bottom of the sleigh.

"I knew this would come in handy,"
he said, proudly.

"Ryder, check out all the presents we found!" Marshall said excitedly.

Ryder looked at the pups. "Skye, I need you and Marshall to drop gifts down chimneys. Zuma, you can deliver gifts to Seal Island. And Chase, I need you to track down those reindeer."

The pups went to work.

Chase used his nose to follow some tracks in the
snow. They led to a reindeer.

"Bingo!" Chase said. "Wait, that's not a reindeer
name. Come here, um, Blitzen?" The reindeer started
to run away. "Donder? Prancer?"

At that, the reindeer stopped. "You guys should
wear name tags," Chase said with a sigh.

Skye zoomed through the chilly air
and swooped in over Katie's Pet Parlour.
She dropped a gift down the chimney.

A few streets away, Marshall tumbled
down Mayor Goodway's chimney and
landed in her living room with a thump.

"Bwok!" squawked Chickaletta, the Mayor's
pet chicken.

"Shhh. Don't wake the Mayor," Marshall
whispered as he put a present under the tree.
Then he slid a gift-wrapped sweetcorn cob over
to the chicken, before going back up the chimney.

Back at the sleigh, Rocky attached the old
ski to the broken runner with a few quick twists
of his screwdriver. But Ryder and the pups still
hadn't found the Magic Christmas Star.

"I have an idea!" Ryder announced. Ryder replayed the Santa Tracker on his PupPad. "This should show us where the star fell."

"It looks like it landed in Farmer Yumi's yard," said Rocky.

"Let's roll!" Ryder exclaimed, and he and the pups ran to their vehicles.

Meanwhile, out on the water, Zuma
guided his hovercraft over the choppy waves.
Wally the Walrus suddenly popped out of
the water, blocking Zuma's path.
"Wally, I have to deliver these presents!"
Zuma yelped.

Zuma tried to motor around Wally,
but the walrus kept getting in his way.
Zuma realized he had a present for Wally.
He found a package shaped like a fish and
tossed it to Wally. "Merry Christmas, dude!"
Wally barked his thanks and moved so
Zuma could speed away.

At Farmer Yumi's barn, Ryder,
Rocky and Rubble were searching
for the Magic Christmas Star.
   Rocky heard Bettina, Farmer
Yumi's cow, mooing.
   They glanced around, but
nobody saw her ... until Ryder
pointed up at the night sky.

Ryder and the pups couldn't believe their
eyes. Bettina was flying through the air –
with the Christmas star stuck to her side!

"The star is making her fly like a reindeer!"
Ryder said.

"How will we get her down?" Rocky asked.

Ryder grabbed some hay and whistled to Bettina. She floated down for her snack. While she was munching the hay, Rocky grabbed the star using a mechanical claw from his Pup Pack.

Ryder quickly called Santa to tell him they'd found the star.

Meanwhile, Chase had found all eight of the reindeer, but they wouldn't line up. He decided that this was a job for his megaphone.

"ATTENTION, ALL REINDEER!" he announced. "Please move forwards in an orderly fashion!" They did as they were told, and Chase led them back to Santa's sleigh.

When Ryder and the pups met at the sleigh,
they found Santa Claus waiting for them.
"My sleigh looks perfect!" Santa exclaimed.
"Except for one missing piece," Ryder said,
holding out the Magic Christmas Star. Santa
took it and hung it on the front of the sleigh.

While the pups loaded the gifts on to Santa's sleigh, Skye playfully took hold of the reins and pretended to be Santa. "I always wanted to sit here! Now dash away, dash away, dash away all!"

The reindeer took off, pulling the sleigh and the pups through the air.

Santa laughed. "Ho, ho, ho! The reindeer always go when they hear that!" He whistled, and the reindeer landed back on the ground. "I don't know how to thank you, Ryder," Santa said. "I thought Christmas would be ruined, but you and the pups have saved it!"

Early the next morning, the pups ran to their Christmas tree. Santa had left gifts for everyone. But before the pups opened theirs, they wanted to give Ryder the present they had picked out just for him – a giant bone!

"It's perfect," Ryder said, laughing. "But I'll tell you what, pups – you can have it. Merry Christmas, everyone!"

The End